STORMY NIGHT

By Robin Wasserman
Illustrated by Duendes del Sur

Hello Reader — Level 1

ISBN 0-439-44418-7

18 17 16   40   11 12 13 14/0

Designed by Maria Stasavage
Printed in the U.S.A.
First printing, March 2003

SCHOLASTIC INC.
New York   Toronto   London   Auckland   Sydney
Mexico City   New Delhi   Hong Kong   Buenos Aires

and were all alone in

the big  .

It was a dark, dark night.

They could not see the or

the .

They could only see the  and

the .

 and sat on the .

They watched .

It was a long, slow night.

Suddenly, flashed.

Thunder crashed.

The lights went out.

 and were all alone in

the big, dark .

"Like, don't be scared, ,"

 said. "I have a ." Shaggy

turned on the . But was

still scared.

So was .

They heard a loud crash in the dining room. Then more noise.

Thud. Thud. Thud.

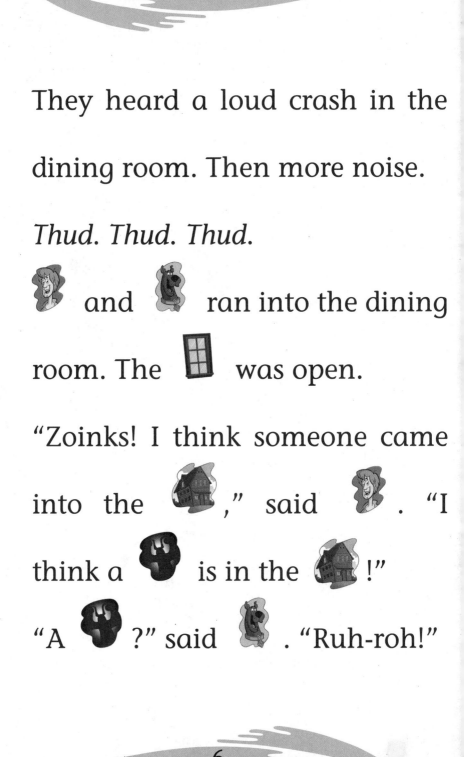 and ran into the dining room. The was open.

"Zoinks! I think someone came into the ," said . "I think a is in the !"

"A ?" said . "Ruh-roh!"

Maybe they were *not* all alone in

the big, dark, scary .

 and ran up the 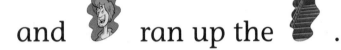 .

They heard noises on the .

Tap, tap. Tap, tap.

"Like, that sounds like footsteps

to me," said.

"Run!" said .

"Hide!" said .

They ran down the .

"Stop!" cried 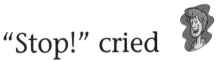 .

There was a dark figure in the living room.

"Zoinks, it's the 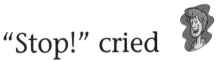 !"

"Run!" yelled 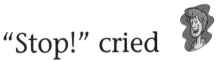 .

"Hide!" shouted 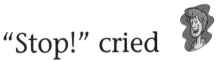 .

They ran into the kitchen.

They shut the .

They were safe now.

They had a snack.

And then . . .

They heard a noise.

Bang.

Bang.

Bang.

Someone was pounding on the back .

Could it be *another* ?

They had nowhere to go.

 hid under the .

 hid under the ⬭.

A 🗝 turned in the lock.

The ⬛ slowly opened.

It was  , , and .

"Why didn't you let us in?"

asked . "We were getting

very wet in the ."

"And why are you hiding?"

asked .

"Shh, ," whispered .

"There's a in the ."

 showed  the  .

"Jinkies," said  . "That's just a  ."

"Why is it so cold in here?" asked 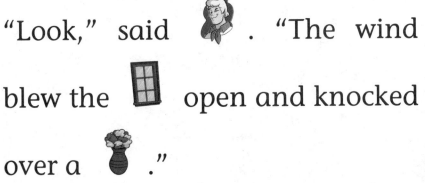 .

"Look," said 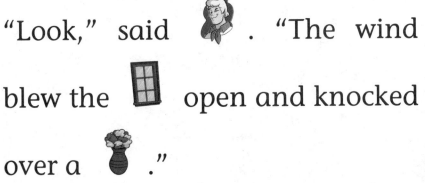 . "The wind blew the 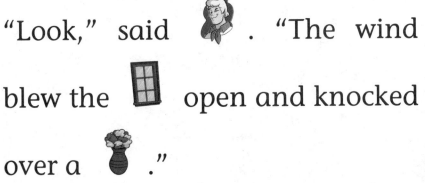 open and knocked over a 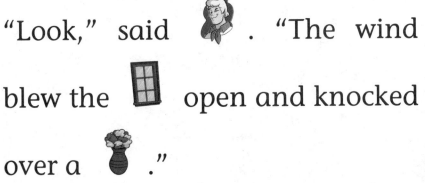 ."

closed the .

 found another  .

 made  and a big

snack.

And they all had a wonderful

night together in the big, dark,

cozy  .

Did you spot all the picture clues in this Scooby-Doo mystery?

Each picture clue is on a flash card. Ask a grown-up to cut out the flash cards. Then try reading the words on the back of the cards. The pictures will be your clue.

Reading is fun with Scooby-Doo!